═══ THE STORY OF ═══
POCAHONTAS,
Indian Princess

BY PATRICIA ADAMS

ILLUSTRATED BY TONY CAPPARELLI

A YEARLING BOOK

ABOUT THIS BOOK

The events described in this book are true. The dialogue has been carefully researched and excerpted from authentic biographies, writings, and commentaries. No part of this biography has been fictionalized.

To learn more about Pocahontas and the Jamestown Settlement, ask your librarian to recommend other fine books you might read.

Published by
Dell Publishing
a division of
Bantam Doubleday Dell Publishing Group, Inc.
666 Fifth Avenue
New York, New York 10103

ISBN: 0-440-47067-6

Published by arrangement with Parachute Press, Inc.
Printed in the United States of America
November 1987

10 9 8 7 6 5 4

CW

Contents

Introduction

ON A BRIGHT APRIL DAY IN 1607 THREE English ships, the *Susan Constant,* the *Godspeed,* and the *Discovery,* sailed into the Chesapeake Bay. On these ships were one hundred men and four boys, who had come to this new land, which they called Virginia, to build a settlement and search for gold.

They moved their ships carefully through the water, looking at the unknown land beyond. Indian scouts watched them from behind the trees.

The Indians had been warned by their prophets that strangers would come to their land and take it away from them.

Were the white men in the big canoes those strangers?

The white men sailed up and down the James River, looking for a place to build their settlement.

The Indians watched from the forest, and waited.

Strangers in the Chesapeake

THE WATER WAS COLD AS POCAHONTAS stepped into the river. Quickly she splashed herself and raised her arms to greet the sun as it rose in the east, over the Chesapeake Bay. She was not alone. With her were many other Indians who had come from surrounding villages. Their morning bath marked the beginning of a special holiday, the day in April when the Algonquian Indians planted the first seeds of the year and honored her father, the great Chief Powhatan.

After her bath Pocahontas tied a sheath made of soft deerskin around her waist. Her head was shaved in front, with a long braid down her back. Pocahontas was eleven, so she was not old enough to let all her hair grow out or wear a full buckskin apron. When she became twelve, she would be considered a young woman and would prepare to marry one of the chiefs in her father's kingdom or even act as an ambassador for Powhatan.

Powhatan was chief of more than ten thousand Algonquian Indians. He had many wives and was the father of many children, but Pocahontas was his favorite daughter. She was a beautiful child with dark, bright eyes and full black hair. Her laugh was merry and she brought pleasure to the people around her. When she was born, she was given a secret tribal name, Matoaka, which may have meant "little snow feather." But as she grew older, she was given the name Pocahontas, which meant "playful," "mischievous," or "frisky."

Pocahontas waited as the Indians planted the corn. First, the men raked the soft spring earth into long rows. The women followed, dropping four grains of corn and two beans into holes dug with sharp wooden tools. Between these holes, squash, pumpkin, and sunflower seeds were pressed into the soil.

Later Pocahontas stood by her father as the Indians gathered to present him with gifts of tribute. Chief Powhatan wore his great raccoon robe, which was sewn with thousands of tiny shells in the shapes of men and animals. The Indians brought him gifts

of meat, bread, furs, and freshwater pearls from the bay. Powhatan gave them gifts, too, beads made of shells, bones, and clay, which they would make into necklaces and bracelets.

At last it was time to play!

The men played a game similar to lacrosse. The women and children played a different ball game. Only the foot could be used to move the ball, and no one was allowed to push or tackle. Pocahontas could run very fast. It never took her long to score a goal.

After the ball game, Pocahontas played tag with her friends. They chased one another until they were exhausted and fell into a laughing heap. That was just like Pocahontas to get everyone laughing! She was always full of pranks and loved to play jokes.

Chief Powhatan must have enjoyed watching his favorite daughter run and play. He was getting old. He had fought many wars and conquered many tribes. He was ready to spend his last years peacefully in his capital village, Werowocomoco, with his family.

Powhatan believed that when he died he

would go beyond the mountains toward the setting sun. There he would remain forever, with his head painted with bright red oil and trimmed with feathers. He would have beads, hatchets, copper, and tobacco, and do nothing but dance and sing with his family. Someday he would be in that land beyond the mountains.

But on this April day he was troubled. News of the white man's arrival had reached Chief Powhatan. He had called a special council meeting to decide what to do about the strangers.

The council meeting took place in Powhatan's longhouse. It was guarded by forty of the tallest warriors in his kingdom. Each guard shaved the right side of his head with sharp shells so that his hair would not get tangled in his bowstring. Many hung a bird's wing or the dried hand of an enemy in the remaining long hair. Inside, seated on a throne of animal skins, Powhatan met with his priests and his *werowance*s, chiefs from smaller villages in his kingdom.

The *werowance*s reported that three great "floating islands" had come into the bay. Once a white "chief" with one arm had come ashore with his men. The Indians had attacked them with their bows and arrows. Although the arrows struck two of the men, they were not killed. Then the white "chief" chased them away with his powerful thunderstick. This thunderstick shot fire over a great distance, farther than an arrow could travel.

The high priest, shaking his headdress of stuffed snake and weasel skins, reminded Powhatan of the prophecy. The prophecy said their land would be invaded by strangers from the east.

How could Powhatan get rid of these strangers? Could the priests develop a magic potion that was more powerful than the thundersticks?

It would take time. The priests would need to spend many days in their temple, tending their eternal fire and praying to the gods. Perhaps it was the evil god Okeus who had brought the white men. Okeus made all the evil in the world, and punished men with sickness, or spoiled their crops with floods, droughts, or other disasters.

Chief Powhatan wanted to know why the white men had come. Did they only want to hunt and fish in the bay or did they want to take Powhatan's land? The *werowance*s were told to learn more about these people.

While the priests tried to discover a magic more powerful than the thundersticks, it was decided that Powhatan's son Pochins would visit the white men. He would show them that they were welcome to hunt and fish. He would do this by giving them baskets of dried oysters, roasted deer, and cakes made from dried corn. He would offer them clay pipes with tobacco. But he would show them that they could not invade Powhatan's kingdom. He would do this by waving his tomahawk and pointing to the land, which meant that there would be war if they tried to take the Indian land.

Late in the day, after the council meeting ended, the Indians gathered for their evening ceremonies. The priests asked the good god Ahone to bless the planting of the corn. Ahone made the sun shine, had created the moon and stars, and made the seeds sprout up from the earth. The priests also prayed that Okeus would not cause the rain to come and wash away the seeds or the hot sun to burn up the corn before the harvest.

Pocahontas sat in a circle with the other

Indians. In the middle of the circle was dried tobacco, an offering to the gods. As the sun dipped behind the trees, casting a shadow across the village, the people raised their hands up toward the sky, singing and chanting. Darkness fell and the air became cool. It was time to end the ceremony.

Pocahontas returned to her father's longhouse, a great house with an arched roof, which was larger than the other lodges of the village. She slept there with her many brothers and sisters. The walls, woven from the tall swamp grass, had been rolled up during the hot day but were let down at night. Inside a fire was burning, with its pleasant smell of smoke and fresh bread cakes.

Overhead the stars shone brightly over the Chesapeake Bay, where the three English ships floated quietly in the night.

Pocahontas had heard of the "floating islands" which had come from far away, across the great water. She had heard the Indian scouts speak of the white men who covered up their entire bodies with heavy cloth and had hair on their faces. Pocahontas had never seen a white man. Perhaps one day she would.

Capture and Rescue

THE WHITE MEN HAD NOT COME TO THE Chesapeake to hunt and fish and then go back to England. They had come to Virginia to stay. When they met with Pochins, they did not understand his sign language, but they did not believe the land belonged to the Indians, anyway. They believed they could claim the land for England, and it would belong to King James.

The ships and supplies for the voyage had been paid for by businessmen in London. These men had put their money together and formed the Virginia Company, which hired men to make the voyage and build a fort on the Chesapeake. These men would be governed by a president and governing council, which was chosen by the Virginia Company. They were to obey their leaders while they searched for gold and other goods to sell in England. They were also to find a new route to the Pacific Ocean and trade with the Indians. The Virginia Company guaranteed that they would have plenty of food and decent houses, and, if the settlement was successful, they would receive money and perhaps become famous back in England.

In May the settlers unloaded their ships on a small peninsula thirty miles by land from Powhatan's capital, Werowocomoco. The captain of the ships, the one-armed Captain Christopher Newport, was liked and respected by the settlers. But he soon left for England to obtain more supplies.

The Virginia Company had designated Edward Wingfield to take over as president of the governing council once Captain Newport left. Under Wingfield's direction the men built a fort which they called Jamestown, in honor of their king. It had a low wall built of tree limbs laid on top of one another. Inside the fort they built some small huts, but many men slept in holes in the earth, with branches pulled over them to keep out the rain.

The settlers had come to Virginia with high hopes. But as the months passed, their hopes turned to despair. They had built their fort in an unhealthy place. The land was low and swampy, with many mosquitoes in the summertime. At high tide the water was too salty to drink, and at low tide it was covered with slime. They had not planted any crops, and the food brought from England had been on the ship so long it was full of worms.

The men became sick, and many of them died of malaria—the "bloody flux," "swellings," and "burning fevers." As the dead bodies were dragged out of the fort to be buried, Indians shot at them from the tall grass. There were no women or children among the settlers, and the men often quarreled and fought with one another.

The men hated their leader, President Edward Wingfield, and would not obey him. They were sure he was eating good food and drinking beer while they were starving.

Most of the men became too sick and hungry to look for gold or explore the rivers. They and the others just wanted to survive until Captain Newport returned from England with more food and supplies.

By August only half of the men who had come to Virginia were still alive. The settlers had built only a few houses, and they had not made friends with the Indians. The governing council decided that President Wingfield did not care enough about his men, and he was replaced by Captain John Ratcliffe. Like Wingfield, however, Ratcliffe was not a good leader. Both were "gentlemen" in England and were not used to the hardships of this new land. Instead of building a prosperous colony, they, too, were sick and hungry and afraid of being killed by the Indians.

There was one man in Jamestown who did not mind the hardships. His name was Captain John Smith. He had been a soldier in Europe and had traveled in North Africa. This small bearded man with bright blue eyes was not afraid of hard work and he was not afraid of the Indians. Most of all, he loved this new land of Virginia.

He wrote in his journal: "Here are mountains, hills, plains, valleys, rivers, brooks, all running most pleasantly into a fair bay, (surrounded by) fruitful and delightsome land. . . . Virginia doeth afford many excellent vegetables, and living creatures . . ."

He wrote of cherries, plums, and large strawberries as well as plentiful deer, squirrel, and raccoon. He saw that the bay was filled with fish and oysters. He learned about the Indians and knew they had plenty of corn and other vegetables.

Captain Smith was enthusiastic and excited about this "delightsome land," and he sent his journals about his adventures in Virginia back to England.

Captain Ratcliffe was angry because John Smith sent his journals to England. Ratcliffe was afraid that Smith would get all the credit and recognition for building the settlement.

Captain Smith did not care what Ratcliffe thought of him. He wanted the Jamestown Colony to survive. The governing council let him take charge of putting the men to work. Smith gave every man who could walk a job. He made sure that the jobs were equal. Some men cut logs and built houses. Others cut down the tall grass to make the thatch, and others put the thatch on the roofs. Before long, not only did each man have a place to live, but the grass around the fort was cut away so Indians could not ambush the settlers.

In the fall the governing council ordered

Captain Smith to go "toward Powhatan" for supplies. He was expected to trade with the Indians and bring food back to the settlement. At the same time he was to explore the many rivers of the bay to see if he could find a water passage to the Pacific Ocean.

Although the Indians were not usually friendly, Smith knew that he had to find ways to seek their help. He needed Indian guides to help him explore the rivers. He also knew that unless the Indians gave the settlers food, they could not survive.

Captain Smith understood the Indian customs better than the other settlers did. He knew that the Indian warriors might kill an ordinary soldier, but they would not kill a white "chief" unless ordered to do so by their leader. He understood that although Powhatan had so far allowed the English to remain at Jamestown, the Indian chief did not want them to stay. Powhatan wanted the white men's weapons for wars with his enemy tribes, but Smith knew if the Indians got weapons, they could also attack Jamestown.

Whenever Smith met with the Indians, he tried to learn words from their language. He used signs and gestures to help make the Indians understand what he was saying. He told them he was a "chief." He also told them that if the Indians gave him food, his soldiers would fight Powhatan's enemies. And if there were any children with the Indians, Smith would always give them toys.

Because of the way Smith talked and behaved with the Indians, he was able to trade glass beads for fish, oysters, bread, turkeys, and corn.

Sometimes, however, Captain Smith would show off his power. If the Indians did not give him food, he would shoot at them and threaten to burn down their villages and take their canoes. Word spread through the tribes that this John Smith was a powerful man. Many Indians said that Smith loved children and his word could be trusted. Other Indians were afraid of Smith and didn't believe him. Captain Smith was aware of how these Indians felt, and he was always ready for attack.

One winter day Captain Smith was traveling up the Chickahominy River. His barge was too large to move far upstream, so he took a canoe and an Indian guide to explore the area. He told his men to stay on the barge with their muskets loaded. He warned them not to go ashore, because the Indians there were unfriendly.

While he was away, however, one of his men, George Cassen, disobeyed the warning. He left the barge and was immediately captured by the Indians.

The warriors tied George Cassen to a tree and began to torture him. First they built a fire, cut off his fingers and toes, and threw them into the flames. Finally they set the tree on fire and did a war dance around George Cassen's burning body.

John Smith was close enough to hear the Indian war cries and to know that he was in deep trouble. Suddenly, out of the woods, over two hundred Indian warriors appeared. John Smith was surrounded! An arrow hit him in the leg but did not hurt him badly. More arrows flew by and some caught in his heavy clothes. Smith fired his gun, but there were too many Indians for one gun.

Desperately he grabbed his Indian guide, using him as a shield. The guide shouted to the other Indians that Captain Smith was a great chief and should not be killed.

Slowly, holding the guide in front of him, Smith began to back away toward the water where his canoe was. Suddenly he began to sink! He had backed into a bog of oozing mud and was stuck up to his knees. He had no choice but to throw his gun and allow the Indians to pull him out of the muck.

Captain Smith's Indian guide kept insisting that Smith was an important chief and could not be killed. The Indians knew of only one chief, the man with one arm. John Smith had to think quickly. He told the Indians that he was Captain Newport's son and should be taken to their chief. The Indians must have believed him, because they put away their weapons and took him to Chief Opechancanough, who was Powhatan's half brother.

Captain Smith stood before Opechancanough with nothing but his bare hands. He began to talk, using every word and gesture he knew in the Indian language.

He said the earth was round, not flat as the Indians thought. He pointed up to the sky and said that the sun chased the night around about the world continuously. He said the world's oceans and rivers were greater than any Indian had ever seen, and there were people of all different colors in the world, not just red or white, but also yellow and black. Opechancanough understood enough to wonder at this man's strange knowledge.

Captain Smith pulled a round object from his pocket. It had a little arrow which pointed in the same direction as he turned the object back and forth. He let Opechancanough try to touch the arrow, but something magic kept his hands from feeling it.

Opechancanough did not know that Captain Smith held a compass and that it was glass that kept his fingers from touching the arrow. Opechancanough thought the compass was a magic instrument. Opechancanough then told Smith that he would be taken to Chief Powhatan.

Captain Smith was very clever. He wrote a long letter which he asked Opechancanough to deliver to Jamestown. Smith said the letter would inform his people he was with the Indians and they were treating him kindly.

The Indians had watched as John Smith wrote strange signs on paper, magic symbols that they did not understand. Would the flat white paper speak to Smith's people in

Jamestown? He was a strange man indeed, a man of power and magic.

For weeks Captain Smith was led from village to village. He did not know what the Indians would do with him. At any moment they might decide to kill him.

The Indians brought him food and danced before him. They wore fox and otter furs. Their skin was painted bright red. Captain Smith was given heavy animal skins to protect him from the winter rain and winds, for it was now December.

More than once the Indians acted like they were going to kill him. But always at the last moment the Indians put away their weapons.

The captain often wondered what the Indians were doing. They gave him many baskets of food and insisted that he eat it all. Were they trying to make him fat so they could cook and eat him?

Finally Smith was brought to Werowocomoco. He was the first white man to see the Indian capital, which was a village on a hill with more than a hundred lodges.

Smith was brought to Powhatan's longhouse, within which several smoking fires burned. When he entered, the smoke burned his eyes, and for a moment he could not see the hundreds of Indians who let out a great shout.

Before a fire Chief Powhatan lay on his throne of animal furs. He had a chain of pearls around his neck, and he wore a great raccoon-skin robe with the tails hanging down from it. On either side of the chief a young woman sat. Also seated nearby were two rows of women and then two rows of men with their heads decorated with feathers, their shoulders painted red.

Powhatan's sister, the queen of the Appomattocs, brought water for Smith to wash his hands and then gave him feathers to dry them. Food was placed before him, and the Indians watched as he ate.

John Smith looked around the smoky room at all the strange faces staring at him as if he were a monster. He was helpless, alone, and without friends.

Among the Indian women sat Pocahontas. She had heard the reports of this white man who had been so brave as he was brought from village to village. She knew he could be tortured and roasted alive on orders from her father.

Pocahontas also knew that a captive could be adopted into the tribe. Indian women could ask for a prisoner to be spared. She was only eleven years old, but as a princess and the favorite daughter of Chief Powhatan, she knew she could ask for this brave man who sat alone before her father.

Powhatan asked Captain Smith questions.

Why had the white men come to his land?

They had been blown here by a storm, the small, bearded Captain Smith answered.

When would they leave?

They were waiting for his father, Captain Newport, to return from England. Then they would leave, Smith tried to explain.

As Pocahontas listened, Chief Powhatan and Captain Smith continued to talk. Using whatever Indian words he knew, the white man told of his own chief, called King James, who had many ships and fierce soldiers with powerful weapons.

Powhatan spoke of fierce tribes who fought against his people.

Pocahontas probably wondered what her father was thinking. Would he put Captain Smith to death? Or would he ask Captain Smith for weapons to fight the enemy tribes?

Finally Powhatan signaled. Two large stones were brought and placed in the middle of the room. The priests began to chant, and the dark room was filled with the sound of voices.

Indians came from the darkened corners and put their hands on Captain Smith, dragging him across the floor and putting his head upon the stones. Two Indians with clubs stood beside him, ready to beat out his brains.

Captain Smith did not try to run. He did not cry or beg for mercy. He was calm, as though he were prepared for death. The dim, smoke-filled room became quiet. Everyone was waiting for Powhatan's command. Suddenly Pocahontas cried out, asking her father to spare the white man. Shouts came from all around, and Powhatan shook his head no.

Pocahontas stood before her father and asked again for Captain John Smith. Powhatan hesitated, but did not agree.

The clubs were raised, and at any moment they would be brought down upon Smith's head. Pocahontas did not ask again, but ran across the floor and threw herself across the kneeling body of Captain Smith. She took

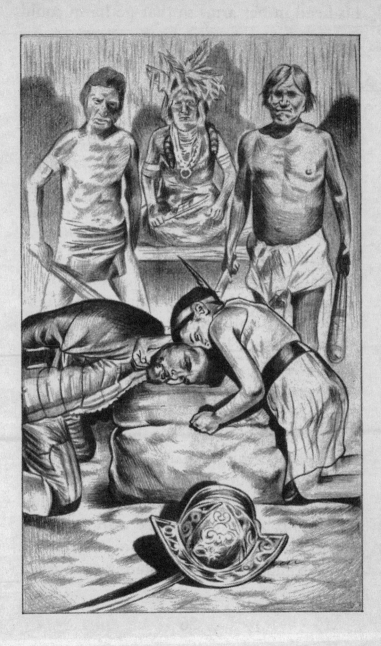

his head in her arms so that no harm could come to him.

Powhatan signaled, and the men with clubs backed away from Captain Smith.

Smith looked up, seeing Pocahontas beside him. He got up from his knees, wondering what had happened. Powhatan explained that his daughter, Pocahontas, wanted Captain Smith to be her brother. He should make her bells, beads, and give her copper trinkets. The captain would now be Powhatan's son and must give him English weapons.

Captain Smith was too relieved to understand exactly what had happened. He knew only that he had been snatched from death by a wonderful little girl, who had thrown herself between him and the horrible clubs. He looked at her and nodded in agreement as her father talked to him.

Pocahontas stood before him, looking at him with her bright dark eyes. She carried herself like a true princess. From now on she would think of John Smith as her brother and would be a friend to the white men.

Perhaps John Smith did not understand that Pocahontas had made him a member of her tribe.

Young Ambassador to Jamestown

NOW THAT POCAHONTAS HAD ADOPTED John Smith, her father expected gifts from the white men. Powhatan sent his aid, Rawhunt, and twelve guards back to Jamestown with Captain Smith to get weapons and a millstone for grinding corn.

John Smith showed the Indians the millstone, but it was much too heavy to move. Then he loaded two cannons with stones and fired them toward the forest. The trees were heavy with ice, which came crashing down with a booming noise. The Indians were amazed and frightened. These weapons were more powerful than anything they had ever seen. Captain John Smith said they could take the cannons. Again, the Indians could not budge them, since they each weighed over three thousand pounds.

Captain Smith said he was sorry that they were unable to take his gifts. Then he gave them bells and other trinkets. The Indians knew they had been tricked, and went unhappily back to Chief Powhatan.

Captain Smith was glad to be safely home after six weeks of captivity. As soon as the Indians left, however, President Ratcliffe told Smith he had been sentenced to death.

How could he be sentenced to death? Captain Smith demanded.

Because two of his men had been killed by the Indians. As their captain, Smith had been responsible for them and was therefore guilty of murder.

John Smith knew that both Wingfield and Ratcliffe hated him. They said he was just an adventurer who wanted to become famous. But Smith realized that both the settlers and the Indians respected him more than they respected Wingfield and Ratcliffe. The Englishmen tried to act like kings, rather than work with their men or spend time with the Indians. John Smith felt *he* was the one who should be giving orders, not Ratcliffe.

But as president, Ratcliffe could order John Smith's execution, and so Smith was sent to the Jamestown jail. The next morning, however, Captain Newport's ship, which was returning from England, was sighted. As soon as Newport heard that John Smith had been sentenced to death, he called for a meeting of the governing council, which set John Smith free.

Captain Newport had brought more settlers from England. They had heard that there was gold in the sandy soil of the Chesapeake Bay and had come to make their fortune.

Everyone wanted gold. If the settlers sent gold back to England, many ships would come to Jamestown with food, supplies, and perhaps even women and children. They would become rich in this new land and have servants to do all the work.

The new settlers thought they saw flecks of gold in the sand by the water. They spent weeks loading sand on a ship returning to England.

Captain John Smith, angry at these men, reported that in Jamestown there was no talk, no hope, no work, nothing but dig gold, wash gold, refine gold, and load gold. While the men loaded "much gilded durt" into bags, the supply of beef, pork, butter, and beer that Captain Newport had brought from England was being eaten up. Before long they would have only a few barrels of wormy barley and some rancid oil to eat.

To make things even worse, a fire broke out in the settlement and many of the buildings were burned. A man who had come to Jamestown with his son lost everything but one mattress.

After the fire Pocahontas made her first trip to Jamestown. She came as an ambassador from her father, bringing fresh meat, corn, and corn bread. Other children from Werowocomoco came with her.

They probably wondered why these men in their burned-out fort were loading bags of sand onto the ships! They probably were amazed at the animals Captain Newport brought back with him. Birds that did not fly away but scratched around in the dirt and laid eggs that could be gathered and eaten every day. Fat animals that wallowed in the mud and could be easily caught and slaughtered. The Indians eventually learned that these animals were called chickens and hogs.

Powhatan sent word through Pocahontas that he wanted to meet John Smith's "fa-

ther," Captain Newport. So in late February of 1608 Captain Smith and Captain Newport went up the river to visit Powhatan. Captain Newport hoped Powhatan would show him where he could find gold. Captain Smith wanted more corn and food.

Captain Newport brought Chief Powhatan gifts from England: a red woolen suit, a "sugarloaf" hat like the king of England wore, and a white greyhound. In addition, Newport "gave" Powhatan a young man, Thomas Savage, who was to live with the Indians and learn their ways. Thomas Savage was only thirteen, but he was brave and strong. He lived with the Indians for many years and became friends with them.

Powhatan was friendly and "gave" the visiting Englishmen one of his servants, Namontack, who would return to England with Captain Newport.

Powhatan wanted the white men's weapons. John Smith was too clever to give him weapons, but perhaps Captain Newport would. Powhatan gave Newport baskets of beans and two hundred and fifty bushels of corn. He said there was a "great water" north of his village, and if the Englishmen would help him fight his enemies, he would show them this water.

Captain Newport was excited to hear this. Perhaps Powhatan would show them a passageway to the Pacific. Captain Newport was ready to promise Powhatan whatever he wished.

Captain Smith said no. They could not spare soldiers to fight Powhatan's enemies. They would have to wait until more settlers arrived.

But Newport gladly agreed to give Powhatan weapons in exchange for the corn and beans. John Smith was quiet. He did not want the Indians to have English weapons. Even though Powhatan had let his daughter Pocahontas adopt him as her brother, John Smith did not trust Powhatan. Powhatan did not trust John Smith, either. He was unhappy that Captain Smith had previously tricked him. Powhatan knew that since more settlers had arrived, he could not expect the white men to leave his land.

But Pocahontas trusted them both—her father and her new brother. She wanted them to be friends, and she hoped the white man could live in peace with her people. She continued to make many trips to Jamestown during the spring and summer. Other children from the Indian village often came with her, carrying turkeys, squirrels, fish, deer, and great loaves of bread.

After the children had delivered the food, they would play games—tag, leapfrog—and sometimes they would do cartwheels. The men and boys in Jamestown enjoyed seeing these cheerful, active Indian children who brought them so much good food.

Captain John Smith was especially delighted with young Pocahontas. He spent many hours with her, teaching her English and learning more words from her language. He wrote down the words she taught him so he could master them. This one sentence he kept with him because he used it so often in speaking with the Indians: *"Kekaten Poka-hontas patiaquagh niugh tanks manotyens mawo-kick rawrenock audaogh."* ("Bid Pocahontas bring hither two little Baskets and I will give her white Beads to make her a Chaine.")

Captain Smith said that it was through Pocahontas's friendship that the men of Jamestown survived that winter. He wrote that next to God, Pocahontas was the most important being that kept the colony from death, famine, and utter confusion.

Although John Smith was grateful to Pocahontas and loved to give her gifts, he was upset when Captain Newport sent twenty swords to Powhatan in exchange for twenty turkeys. Captain Smith knew the Indians could use these weapons to attack the Jamestown settlement. When Captain Newport returned to England again, John Smith refused to send Powhatan more weapons. Glass beads and copper, but no weapons. This made Powhatan angry.

Just as John Smith had feared, the Indians began to use the swords Captain Newport had given them to attack settlers when they were outside the fort, taking more weapons from them.

This had to stop. Captain Smith was not going to let the Indians steal weapons. With the white man's weapons the Indians could kill all the settlers.

To show the Indians he would not let them take weapons, Smith captured seven Indians and threw them into the Jamestown jail. He threatened to torture them and fired his musket above their heads, which frightened them more than the thought of having their fingers and toes cut off and burned.

Before long Pocahontas came to Jamestown, bringing gifts from her father. Pocahontas stood before John Smith and said that her father loved and honored him. She did not ask for the release of the other Indians because, as a princess, she would never beg.

John Smith could see how Pocahontas was growing up and how proudly she held herself as she spoke. She undertook her duties as an ambassador for her father very seriously. He finally agreed to turn the captured Indians over to "Pocahontas, the King's Daughter."

Once again this young girl had made it possible for grown men to make peace with one another.

The Midnight Rescue

AFTER CAPTAIN SMITH RETURNED THE Indian prisoners to Powhatan, Pocahontas continued to bring gifts to Jamestown. Life was better that summer of 1608. The men were not so hungry. But they still thought more about gold than about planting.

In the fall the governing council elected John Smith president of Jamestown. At last he might be able to make this settlement a success. He made all the men work together, instead of arguing about who was more important or where there was gold. He insisted that the men fish and plant crops so they would not have to depend on the Indians for food.

Everyone worked. The church was repaired, a new roof was put on the storehouse, and everyone in the colony practiced military drills each Saturday.

Captain Newport returned from England

in the fall of 1608. He brought with him seventy new colonists, including two women, and instructions from the Virginia Company for President Smith. He must send gold to England, have the settlers make tar and glass, and find a route to the Pacific. John Smith was furious! There was no gold in the Chesapeake and probably no route to the Pacific. His men needed to build houses, plant, and fish, not make tar and glass.

Another order made him even angrier. Captain Newport had brought a great English bed, a copper crown, and a red woolen robe to present to the Indian chief, and Captain Smith was to "crown" Powhatan. The men of the Virginia Company in England had decided that if Powhatan were crowned like the English king and given a big bed, he would obey the white men.

John Smith knew the great Powhatan would obey no white man. Such fine gifts would only make him refuse to take copper and beads in exchange for bushels of corn.

Captain Newport insisted that the crowning take place, however, and sent Captain Smith to Werowocomoco to invite the chief to Jamestown for his coronation.

When Smith arrived at Werowocomoco, he was told that Powhatan was a day's journey away at another village. Messengers were sent to get Powhatan while Smith waited.

Pocahontas was at Werowocomoco, and she welcomed Smith and his men. She led them to a field, where she built a fire and brought mats for them to sit on. Men, women, and children sat around the fire with them.

Suddenly the air was filled with shrieking. Captain Smith was sure that Powhatan had laid a trap for him. Quickly he grabbed his musket. Pocahontas put one hand on her heart and raised the other toward the sun. She swore that Smith would not be hurt. If anything bad happened, he could kill her, she told him.

Captain Smith trusted Pocahontas, and so he sat back down on his mat. Pocahontas disappeared for a while, and then about thirty young women came running out of the forest. Their bodies were brightly painted in different colors, and they were naked except for skirts made of green leaves. Captain Smith recognized Pocahontas as the leader. She wore a pair of big horns on her head and otter skins across her arm. She had a quiver of arrows on her back, with bow and arrows in her hand. Behind her the other young women also wore horns and carried swords, wooden spoons, and clubs.

The young women danced and sang, leaping around the fire for over an hour. Smith and his men did not know what to make of this celebration. To the Englishmen, their songs were "hellish shouts and cries" and "infernal passions." For the Indian girls it was a celebration of the harvest.

After the dancing and singing the young women brought the white men into a great lodge, where they gave them fresh bread and meat. Then they skipped around the men, asking, in the English that Pocahontas had probably taught them, "Love you not me?"

Pocahontas entertained her guests in the royal tradition of an Indian princess. As Captain Smith watched her dance, sing, and lead the other young women, he must have realized that the little girl who had played and run around the fort, was growing up.

When Powhatan returned to Werowoco-moco the next day, Captain Smith invited him to Jamestown to receive the gifts from the king of England and "Father" Newport.

Powhatan shook his head and said: "If your King have sent me presents, I also am a King, and this is my land: eight days I will stay to receive them. Your Father is to come to me, not I to him, nor yet to your fort, neither will I bite at such a bait."

Powhatan was wary of the white men, and he was tired of their gifts. They would only give him glass beads and bits of copper, which were useless if the Indians gave away all their food. He wanted only weapons.

Since Powhatan refused to go to Jamestown, Captain Newport and Captain Smith loaded the large bed, robe, crown, and other furniture onto a barge and traveled the eighty miles by water to Werowocomoco. Dressed in their finest clothes, they marched into Powhatan's longhouse. He received them lying on his throne of animal skins. He watched solemnly as they assembled the large canopy bed and placed jugs, basins, and a pitcher before him.

Then they held up the coronation robe for him to put on. At first Powhatan shook his head. He did not want this robe across his shoulders. It might have some evil magic in it. Finally he put on the robe but then refused to kneel to be crowned. He was a king, and he had never bent his knees to any man.

Someone behind Powhatan pressed down upon his shoulder, and before he could straighten up, Captain Newport quickly placed the crown on his head.

Powhatan, the mighty chief, stood before the white captains. He was wearing their robe and their crown, but he would never obey them.

In response to his coronation Powhatan handed over his buckskin robe and an old pair of moccasins to Captain Newport to give to his king. Then he said he would send seven baskets of corn back to Jamestown.

Seven baskets of corn! That was nothing! Captain Smith knew that Powhatan no longer respected the settlers. This coronation had been a joke.

John Smith was troubled as he left Werowocomoco. Winter was coming and more settlers were in Jamestown. Although some work had been done, under John Smith's leadership, he said many of the new settlers were "the scumme of the world." Most of the people spent their time searching for gold. It was up to John Smith to find food for everyone.

Powhatan had sent Pocahontas to the fort throughout their first winter of 1608, but would he do so again? Smith had his doubts. Even though Pocahontas was John Smith's friend, she could not disobey her father.

Another winter came, and the Indians who had once been friendly now refused to trade for food. John Smith was sure that Powhatan had given orders to the Indians to "starve out" the white men.

Then, during the first cold months of 1609, Powhatan invited John Smith to visit him in Werowocomoco. He promised a boatload of corn in exchange for an English house, a grindstone, copper and beads, fifty swords, some guns, a rooster, and a hen.

John Smith sent men ahead to Werowocomoco to begin building Powhatan his house. He packed up some copper and beads and started out to meet with the chief. He knew Pocahontas would be with her father, and because of her he probably felt safe, even though he expected Powhatan might be laying a trap for him.

When John Smith and his men arrived in

Powhatan's longhouse, the chief acted surprised that they had come.

"You invited me," John Smith said, "and offered me a boatload of corn."

"We have little corn," Powhatan said. "My people will go hungry this winter. But, for forty swords, I can spare forty baskets of corn."

"I will give you copper," Smith answered.

"My people cannot eat copper," Powhatan said. "Without corn, we may go hungry."

"Out of my love for you, Powhatan," Smith said, "I have sent men to build you a house, even when we needed these men in Jamestown. I am sorry you cannot give me corn. I can only ask for it. I would never steal or break our friendship ... except if you force me to by your bad treatment."

Powhatan was angry. "Captain Smith," he said, "many do inform me, your coming hither is not for trade, but to invade my people, and possess my country."

Powhatan realized that the white men planned to stay in the Chesapeake. The chief was impatient with the Englishmen and their constant demands for more and more food. Soon they would want more land as well. And no matter what he gave them, they refused to give the weapons he needed.

Perhaps Powhatan thought again about the prophecy, and he realized that if these men weren't forced to leave, they would take his land from him and his people.

For hours Smith and Powhatan spoke with each other. Powhatan insisted that as one of his "chiefs" and his son, Captain Smith should obey him. Smith answered that he only obeyed God and King James.

Powhatan told Smith that he wanted no more war, he wanted only to live peacefully with his family in his own house. With that, he agreed to give Smith some corn. Then he slipped out of the room and disappeared.

Captain Smith thought it strange that Powhatan had left so quickly. Where had Powhatan gone? Where was Pocahontas? Captain Smith felt uneasy as he sat by the fire. In spite of the talk of peace and friendship, he could feel that something was wrong.

Captain Smith waited for Indians to bring corn, but none came. He went to check his barge. The tide had gone out and it was stuck in the mud. He decided to wait in a wigwam in Werowocomoco until the tide came in.

Indians could be seen around the wigwam, and there was movement in the village. Something was going on, but what? Captain Smith could not figure out what it was.

That night there was a knock on the entrance to the lodge. Outside stood Pocahontas, her body shivering. It was bitter cold, with snow falling in the darkness.

She told John Smith that she had run many miles through the forest, from her father's special hideout. Powhatan had taken her there with him because his warriors were planning to kill John Smith and his men.

As she stood there, so cold and frightened, John Smith wanted to thank her for saving his life again. He took some glass beads from his pocket and offered them to her as a token of appreciation. She shook her head, no. Tears began to run down her cheeks.

"If my father would see me with these gifts, he would kill me," she said, and, still crying, still wet, she turned from Captain John Smith and ran off alone into the dark, cold night.

Two Friends Part

AFTER POCAHONTAS'S WARNING, CAP-
tain Smith escaped from Werowocomoco. Soon after, another white man,
Richard Wiffin, came looking for him. Pocahontas knew that if her father's guards found
Wiffin, he would be killed. She sneaked him
into a hideout and gave him warm food and
dry clothes. When the Indian guards came
looking for Richard Wiffin, she told them he
had run off, through the forest. As soon as it
was safe, she helped him escape.

Later Pocahontas convinced Powhatan's
warriors not to kill Henry Spelman, a young
white man who, like Thomas Savage, had
been "given" to the Indians.

Pocahontas was very brave to help John
Smith and the other men, for Powhatan had
decided that the white men were his enemies.
Anyone who helped them was a traitor and
could be killed. Even his favorite daughter.

Powhatan moved with his family to a village called Orapaks, which was hidden deep in the forest. Here his family would be safe from the Englishmen, for Powhatan planned to wage war against them. Pocahontas was no longer allowed to visit the English settlement. She was not to see Smith or be his friend.

Pocahontas must have felt sad that her father and her adopted brother, John Smith, were no longer friends. She could no longer go to Jamestown to take gifts to the white men. She could no longer spend hours learning English and teaching John Smith Indian words. She could only learn about Jamestown from Powhatan's scouts.

Many Indians tried to kill Captain Smith as he traveled back to Jamestown. They tried to ambush him, but he was too clever to be caught. Once, when he had fallen asleep in the forest, an Indian snuck up on him with his tomahawk raised. John Smith woke up just in time and chased him away. Another Indian tried to poison him, but John Smith threw up the poison before it killed him.

The Indians began to believe that Smith had some special magic. Once, Smith arrested two Indian brothers because they had stolen a gun. He put one in the Jamestown jail and told his brother that if he returned the gun by morning, they could both go free.

It was very cold, so a charcoal fire was built in the prison cell. The next morning the prisoner was found badly burned and almost dead from the fumes. John Smith tried to revive him with brandy and water, which made him conscious again but very drunk. His brother was terrified. He thought his body had come back alive but was now possessed with a devil. Smith promised he would get rid of the devil. After a good sleep the prisoner was fine. When the gun was returned, Smith released the two brothers. They told the Indians what had happened. John Smith could bring dead people back alive!

During the spring and summer of 1609 Captain Smith took on the task of fixing up the settlement. The other members of the governing council had been killed when their boat capsized, and now Smith was completely in charge. He insisted every man work, whether he wanted to or not. Smith was very strict and punished anyone who was lazy.

A deep well was dug and finally Jamestown had fresh water. New roofs were put on the buildings and a new storehouse built. Nets were made for fishing and crops were planted. The hogs were put on an island where they would be safe, and soon there were over sixty of them. The chickens multiplied to more than five hundred.

A glass factory was built, tar and soap were made, and trees were cut down for lumber. The corn was harvested and put in the storehouse for winter. There would be enough food now without having to trade with the Indians. At last it seemed as though the Jamestown settlement was going to be successful.

Then a terrible thing happened. One day a man went into the storehouse to get corn and found thousands of rats! Some had come over on the ships from England and had multiplied. Most of the corn was ruined. Once again the colony faced a winter of hunger.

John Smith knew he could no longer depend on the Indians for food. Their corn had not grown well that year, and they themselves had little to eat.

He decided to do what the Indians did when food was scarce. He divided the colony into three groups. One group went down to an island where they could catch fish and oysters. Another group was sent into the forest to gather acorns and wild berries. The third group was sent to live with friendly Indians. The colonists learned to make bread from tuckahoe roots. They hunted wild animals and even learned to dry fish and mix fish eggs (roe) with wild grass for food. Over the winter only six people out of two hundred died. John Smith had finally taught the Englishmen how to live in this new land.

The settlers still did not get along among themselves, however. They argued about who was doing the most work and were angry when John Smith punished them. Some wanted to trade their kettles, tools, and even swords with the Indians rather than work for their food. This discouraged John Smith. He wrote that some would rather "have starved or have eaten one another" than work.

In July of 1609 ships arrived from England with hundreds of new settlers. The Virginia Company in London had appointed new men to run the colony. The men in London did not even appreciate all the work Captain Smith had done. He was told that he was no longer president.

One day in September John Smith was returning to Jamestown after a long trip upriver. He lay down in his boat to take a nap. A spark from someone's pipe alighted on Smith's gunpowder bag, and suddenly it burst into flames. John Smith's clothes caught fire, and he jumped into the water and had to be rescued from drowning. As his men placed him in the boat, they could see that he was badly burned.

John Smith's wounds did not heal quickly and he was in great pain. He knew he could get good medical treatment from doctors in London. Also, after two years of struggling to make the settlement successful, he was disheartened and tired of the bickering and fighting in Jamestown. He asked to be taken on board a ship that was leaving for England. And so John Smith left Virginia, the land he had grown to love.

It was autumn, the time for harvest feasting and celebration. During the last harvest Pocahontas and her friends had performed for Captain Smith. That had been a happy time, when her people and the white men were friends. After visiting the settlers so often and risking her life twice to save them, it must have been difficult for Pocahontas to stay in her father's isolated Indian village.

On a cool day, when the sun was low in the southern sky, an Indian spy came to Powhatan. He brought news of John Smith. A terrible fire had burst forth upon Smith's body, and he had burned to death.

No! It could not be! Surely the spy was mistaken. How could Smith burst into flames? Did gods punish him for some wrongdoing?

Pocahontas had not seen Smith since that night when she had run through the dark forest to warn him. Now she believed he was dead. Pocahontas felt a great sadness. She could not hope to be with him again.

Pocahontas was almost fourteen years old. Her father wanted her to remain with the Indians and have nothing to do with the white men. With John Smith gone, perhaps Pocahontas did not want to return to the white man's world. Perhaps she felt her life with them was over.

Kidnapped!

WITHOUT JOHN SMITH TO LEAD THE colony, everything went wrong. The winter of 1609–10 came, and again there was not enough food. The Indians refused to give the settlers more corn, and the men began to rob one another. When they had eaten whatever food they had, they killed the dogs and cats and ate them. They were still starving, so they killed and ate the rats who had eaten their corn.

John Smith was right when he wrote that the people would rather "have starved or eaten one another" than work. Without his leadership they became desperate. An Indian was killed and his flesh roasted and eaten. A man dug up his dead wife and cooked and ate her.

If anyone sneaked out of the fort to search for snakes or roots to eat, the Indians attacked them. Even so, some of the settlers ran off and begged the Indians to let them live with them. By the end of the winter there were only sixty people left at the settlement—from over five hundred.

Those few settlers wanted to leave Jamestown. Since John Smith had returned to England, they had seen nothing but trouble. War had been declared by Powhatan, and the Indians seemed determined to wipe out every white man who remained. Instead of Pocahontas bringing food to the fort, Indians shouted taunts from the woods, like: *"Yah ha ha Tewittaw Tewittaw."* ("Each death, another gun.")

In the spring of 1610 two more ships arrived from England, the *Deliverance* and the *Patience*. As the new settlers disembarked from their ships, they found the walls of the fort collapsing and the houses empty. The doors and shutters had been pulled off and burned for firewood.

The ships contained only a month's supply of food. It was May, the time for planting, not harvesting. There was no hope of trading for food with the Indians. The captain of the ships, Sir Thomas Gates, decided to return to England and to take the Jamestown survivors with him.

The settlers packed up the few things they had and climbed onto the *Patience* and the *Deliverance*. After their terrible winter they were glad to leave. Let the Indians have it, they thought. Jamestown had brought nothing but misery, hunger, and death.

Just as the two ships were sailing through the bay, headed for the open water of the Atlantic Ocean, they spotted three more English ships arriving. They were commanded by Lord De La Warr, a leader of the Virginia Company who had decided to come to Virginia to govern Jamestown himself. He ordered the *Deliverance* and the *Patience* to turn around.

Lord De La Warr felt, as Captain Smith had, that the colony had failed because the men were lazy. He had brought plenty of food so no one needed to starve. He immediately, however, put everyone to work to rebuild Jamestown.

Lord De La Warr was a good leader of the white men, but he did not understand the Indians as John Smith did. He thought they were all savages and must do whatever he said. He sent a message to Powhatan to return all the stolen weapons or else. Powhatan answered that if the white men didn't stay inside the Jamestown fort, he would have them all killed.

The Indians and the white men began to fight regularly. Indians captured many men and tortured them to death. The new settlers burned Indian villages and destroyed Indian crops. Once the white men captured Pocahontas's aunt and her children, and brought them onto their boat. As one of the soldiers later wrote, "it was agreed upon to put the children to death, ... by throwing them overboard and shooting out their brains in the water." Afterward, they killed the mother.

Pocahontas knew that her father had declared war on the settlement, and she must have heard of the cruelty on both sides. Nevertheless, she continued to help white men escape from Powhatan's warriors. Powhatan, perhaps seeing that his daughter still wanted to be friends with the white settlers, sent her away from Orapaks. She went to a village of the Potomac Indians, as far away as she could be from Jamestown and still be with friendly Indians.

During the three years Pocahontas lived

with the Potomac Indians, the Jamestown settlement grew. Hundreds of new settlers arrived from England and more forts were built in the Chesapeake. Although she must have heard of the activities of the white men, she had no further contact with them until she was seventeen years old.

Pocahontas was living with the Potomac chief, Japazaws, when Samuel Argall, the captain of an English ship, came to the Potomac country on a trading mission from Jamestown. After meeting with Argall, Japazaws told Pocahontas she had been invited onto the boat to see it. Pocahontas must have been very curious to see the white men after such a long time away from Jamestown. Perhaps some white men on the boat had been in Jamestown when she had delivered meat and bread there four years ago. Perhaps someone on board had also known Captain John Smith.

Her father was still at war with the white men. To disobey him again could be very dangerous for Pocahontas. She told Japazaws that she could not go on the boat.

Japazaws's wife then told her husband that *she* wanted to visit the ship. Japazaws said no, a woman was not allowed to go alone onto the white man's boat. She made a great fuss, begging her husband to let her go on board until he threatened to beat her to make her be quiet. She cried and said how very much she wanted to see this boat up close. Finally Japazaws said he would allow her to go only if Pocahontas went too.

Pocahontas hesitated. She was a princess and should obey her father, the chief. But the ship was so close! She had been separated from her white friends for so long! Perhaps Pocahontas thought that nothing bad could happen if she just went on board for a little while. Japazaws said it was all right for her to go, and he was her friend and also a chief.

Pocahontas finally agreed. When they boarded the boat, Captain Argall introduced himself. He said he had heard wonderful things about her. He invited Pocahontas, Japazaws, and his wife to sit with him at his table, and he served them delicious food. Pocahontas looked around the ship's room, at the wooden seats, the rugs, books, and navigation instruments. The white man's world was really very interesting. There were still so many things to learn.

Was Pocahontas tired? Captain Argall asked. There was a nice little room where she could rest for a while. Then she would be taken back to shore.

Pocahontas agreed to rest in this room. Perhaps she wanted to feel the bed, the soft cloth on it, and to look at the pictures and touch the glass in the little round window.

After she had been in the room only a few minutes, Pocahontas heard Japazaws and his wife shouting. She ran up to the deck where Captain Argall was ordering them off the boat.

When Pocahontas tried to join them, Captain Argall blocked her way. She cried out to her friends, and they shouted and waved in protest as they got into their canoe. Then, as the canoe moved away from the English boat, Japazaws and his wife took out a brand-new copper kettle and some bright beads. They laughed as they held the kettle up to see their prize better.

What was happening? Pocahontas looked around in confusion. Captain Argall explained that she was now a hostage and

would be taken to Jamestown. Her father had captured eight Englishmen and stolen many weapons. Pocahontas could return to her father when he gave the weapons back and set the Englishmen free.

Pocahontas had been tricked by Japazaws and his wife! They had planned this hoax with Captain Argall to get her on his boat. She had been traded for a copper kettle! Her own people had betrayed her.

She looked at the men on the boat. She did not know them. She had always felt safe and protected with Captain John Smith, but what would these sailors do to her? Perhaps they would torture her, like her own people sometimes did to hostages.

Pocahontas began to cry. What was going to happen to her? Would her father return the captives and the weapons he had stolen? She knew how important weapons were for her father. But she also knew her father was getting old and had said he was tired of fighting. He wanted to live in peace with his family. Perhaps he would send the ransom soon so she could return to her people.

She did not know what Jamestown was like now. She had gone there as a child, carrying gifts and playing leapfrog or learning English from John Smith. But she was no longer a child. John Smith was gone, and these people were strangers.

The men on the ship smiled and bowed to her. Captain Argall spoke kindly to her in words that she could understand. He told her that she would be well treated in Jamestown because she was a royal princess.

Pocahontas knew she would be with the white women who had come from England, and she could learn more English from them. She would see the new buildings and meet the many people. Bravely Pocahontas turned toward Jamestown.

A New World

JAMESTOWN WAS VERY DIFFERENT FROM the village that Pocahontas had visited four years before. Lord De La Warr had left and Sir Thomas Dale was the governor. He was a harsh man who severely punished the settlers for the slightest wrongdoing. He called his rules the "Laws Devine, Morall, and Martiall." The settlers called them "Laws of Blood."

If a man cursed, he was beaten with a whip. If he cursed again, his tongue was punched full of holes. If he dared curse again, he was killed. If anyone missed church, he was beaten. If he took someone else's corn, he could have his ears cut off.

Although the settlers were unhappy with Dale's rules, they dared not disobey. Jamestown became an industrious town with many houses, a new church, vegetable gardens, and fields of corn. New forts were built along the riverbanks. The people were set to work cutting trees for lumber and making bricks.

Many women and children now lived in Jamestown. Flowers grew in the yards and chickens and pigs ran around. There were few people left from the days of Pocahontas's visits, but the new people had heard of her.

When she arrived with Captain Argall, they did not treat her as a captive but as a new friend. They wanted to teach her more English and show her how to sew and to cook English food and to sing English songs.

Life with these people was very different from life with the Indians. The women wore many layers of cloth which covered up their bodies and dragged along the ground. Pocahontas let them dress her so that she looked like they did. She did not want to be the only young woman in Jamestown dressed in a loose buckskin apron!

Pocahontas was told that she would not stay in Jamestown. She would go to a new fort called Henrico. Here, her father's warriors would not be able to rescue her.

In Henrico she lived with Reverend Whitaker, who had come to Virginia to convince the Indians to become Christians. He believed that worshiping Okeus and Ahone was devil worship, and the Indian "savages" should be taught to worship one god.

Reverend Whitaker soon realized that Pocahontas was no "savage." He was kind to her and gave her a nice soft bed and good things to eat. Saturday nights he taught her the rules of his religion. Sunday mornings she went with him to church, where people gathered to sing and to listen to Reverend Whitaker speak. On Sunday afternoons he taught her Bible verses. He taught her the alphabet and soon she could recognize these strange letters and read words.

It was like magic, what Reverend Whitaker showed her! The people were pleased when she read and recited Bible verses.

Pocahontas must have thought a lot about the Christian religion. These people, who could cross the great water in big canoes and make thundersticks and build houses with many rooms, believed in one god. Perhaps their god was the right god and her gods of good and evil were wrong.

She was not sure at first. But the longer she stayed with the white men, the more she believed that they were right.

Meanwhile, word was sent to Powhatan that his daughter had been kidnapped. He sent some corn and a few broken weapons and said he hoped Pocahontas was well treated.

A few broken swords and some corn? Pocahontas could not have forgotten how her father had said that he loved her better than his own life. Now he sent only one canoe full of corn and seven swords for her ransom!

Even if her father paid the ransom, Pocahontas may have asked herself if she truly wanted to go back and live with her Indian relatives. Perhaps it was better here with these people who read these magic words and spoke of love and forgiveness. They talked of another life, a life after death. There she might see Captain Smith again and talk to him about their time together.

Month after month Pocahontas stayed with her new friends, but Powhatan did not pay the ransom for his daughter. She was becoming used to the ways of the English settlers. She had even learned to walk comfortably in a long skirt. She still preferred to wear her old Indian moccasins, however.

After living in Jamestown for almost a

year, Pocahontas agreed to be baptized. At her baptism she was given a new name from the Bible, Rebecca. This was her third name. She had left her Indian home and no longer used her Indian names, Matoaka and Pocahontas. She was now an eighteen-year-old Christian woman in the white man's world.

One man watched Pocahontas attentively as she read aloud from her Bible and sang hymns in the church. He spent many hours in Reverend Whitaker's house, where Pocahontas lived. His name was John Rolfe, and he had come to Jamestown to start a farm. He had been married, but his wife and child had died on the trip from England.

Pocahontas understood John Rolfe better than the men who had only hunted for gold. Rolfe, like her own people, planted seeds and watched for the dark clouds to bring rain. He was grateful for the summer sun which ripened his crop before the harvest.

He planted tobacco, the sacred plant of the Indians. John Rolfe took good care of his plants and grew tobacco that was even finer than the Indian tobacco that Pocahontas knew.

He told her he cared for her and wanted

71

to marry her. Pocahontas saw that this man was kind and he loved her. Perhaps he reminded her of John Smith. She agreed to marry him.

Since John Rolfe was the first white man to marry an Indian, he had to ask Sir Thomas Dale for permission. He insisted that Pocahontas was a good woman and was a Christian, not a savage. He admitted that her manners were sometimes strange and she did not have a good education, but he loved her so much that he could think only of her day and night.

Thomas Dale decided it was a good idea for John Rolfe to marry Pocahontas. He admired this proud and beautiful Indian woman, and wasn't she also an Indian princess? If she were married to a white man, perhaps Powhatan would be more friendly to the settlers and return the weapons.

In March of 1614, a year after Pocahontas was kidnapped, Sir Thomas Dale made a final attempt to obtain the ransom from Chief Powhatan. Dale took Pocahontas, John Rolfe, and one hundred and fifty men on his ship upriver toward Powhatan's village.

Powhatan had sent two sons to visit Pocahontas on Sir Dale's ship. Pocahontas had not seen anyone from her Indian family in over a year. She was friendly to her brothers, but withdrawn. They asked her if she was being well treated, and she answered that she was fine. Then she said that she wanted to remain with her friends in the white village because her father loved his old swords, guns, and axes better than he loved her. With that, she turned away from her Indian brothers.

Governor Dale told the brothers that John Rolfe wished to marry Pocahontas. Soon Powhatan sent a message back to Dale; he agreed that Pocahontas should marry John Rolfe. He said he would return the stolen weapons in fifteen days, and if any Indian stole from the settlers again, he would be punished. He wanted to be friends with Governor Dale and hoped the governor would treat Pocahontas as his own daughter.

In the spring, seven years after Captain John Smith came to Chesapeake Bay, Pocahontas took another Englishman into her heart. She agreed to love, honor, and obey John Rolfe as his wife. They were married in the new church in Henrico. Powhatan did not attend because he had vowed never to go to the English settlement. He sent Pocahontas a pearl necklace and gave her and John Rolfe land for their tobacco farm.

By now Pocahontas had left her life among the Indians for good. She would never again roam the dark forests or fish the shallow waters with her cousins. She would never again even see her father, the aging man who had watched her dance and play as a little girl. Her Indian father was now a part of her past, just as John Smith was a part of her past. She was now a woman who would stand by her husband, help him plant his tobacco, have his children, and go with him wherever he went.

By choosing to marry John Rolfe, she had saved many people—both Indians and whites—from senseless death and slaughter. While Pocahontas and John Rolfe lived in Virginia, their people lived in peace. For years afterward this time in the New World would be remembered as "The Peace of Pocahontas." But this was not to last!

The Trip to England

WHEN THE ENGLISHMEN OF THE VIRginia Company paid for the ships to go to Virginia, they hoped the settlers would find gold and a way to the Pacific Ocean. Gold was never found, and there was no water route from Virginia to the Pacific. It was tobacco, first grown by John Rolfe, which finally brought money to the settlement.

The Indians considered tobacco a sacred plant which they offered to their gods and smoked during special ceremonies. The white men had tried the tobacco in the Indians' pipes and decided that they liked the sweet, rich taste very much. In England men were wanting more tobacco, and John Rolfe could sell everything he planted.

He and Pocahontas lived on the land that had been given to them by Powhatan. Soon after they were married, they had a baby boy, Thomas. Pocahontas was very busy, helping her husband with the tobacco and caring for her baby. She lived in a nice home, where her Indian cousins and friends were welcome to visit.

Pocahontas was talked about even far away in England. People wanted to know more about this Indian princess who had become a Christian, married an Englishman, and given birth to his son. They wanted to see this woman who they had heard was so beautiful, in her Indian way, that an English gentleman had fallen madly in love with her.

The Virginia Company sent money for John Rolfe and his wife to come to England. Pocahontas had heard John Smith speak of England. She had heard of the great village of London, where people lived on top of each other in tall houses. She had heard of many horses pulling coaches and narrow streets filled with wagons and people selling bright cloth and jewelry. Pocahontas was willing to travel across the great water, and she wanted some of her own friends and relatives to go with her.

In April 1616, nine years after the first English ships arrived in Virginia, Pocahontas left her country for England. Twelve

Indians, including Pocahontas's half sister Matachanna and her husband, Tomocomo, traveled with her. Tomocomo came on board with his body brightly painted, wearing a breechcloth made of an animal's head and tail, and a fur cape. Tomocomo also brought with him a long stick for counting English people. He planned to carve a notch in the stick for every Englishman he saw.

No matter what John Rolfe or Captain Smith had told Pocahontas of London, she could not have been prepared for the busy, noisy city she saw when she arrived. She had never seen so many streets and houses and people. There were even stores and houses built on London bridge itself! The Indians, who had only heard the sounds of the crickets and other night animals after dark, must have been amazed at the clanging bells and the sounds of horses' hooves on the street all night. There were far too many people for Tomocomo to count on his stick.

Everyone wanted to see the Indian princess. Many people came by the inn where she was staying just to look at her and her young son. Whenever she walked on the streets or attended a party or the theater,

people would stop and look at her. Sometimes they pointed and called out, "Look at
the Indian," even though she was dressed
just like they were.

She was taken to meet the bishop of London, and one day a fancy coach brought her
to meet King James and his wife, Queen
Anne. It must have been exciting to visit the
king and queen and see the many beautiful
lords and ladies in their fine clothes.

Pocahontas, who was often called by her
English name, Lady Rebecca, walked
proudly among these lords and ladies and
spoke carefully and correctly with them.
One man wrote that she "carried herself as
the daughter of a king." Everyone spoke of
how fine this Indian woman was . . . why,
she did not seem like a savage at all!

With her Indian relatives she was still Pocahontas. Together they would show
Thomas the horses as they trotted up the
narrow London streets or watch the acrobats
in the square doing flips and somersaults . . .
just like she had done as a young girl.

In London Pocahontas made a discovery.
Captain John Smith was alive! He had not
been killed after all, but had returned to

England and recovered from his wounds. He had written Queen Anne a long letter telling her of his friend Pocahontas. He had said that she had "hazarded the beating out of her own brains to save mine," and had risked her life more than once to save him. He wrote that she had been the most important person, next to God, for the Jamestown settlement.

John Smith had written to the queen of England about Pocahontas, but he had not walked the small distance to find her in London.

Day after day, month after month, Pocahontas had waited for John Smith to knock on her door. Everywhere she looked for him, on the street, at the court of the king and queen, and in the coaches going by.

Why had he not come? She didn't understand. He was, after all, her very own adopted brother. The man she had saved and who had first told her about England and London.

London was damp and there was heavy smoke in the air when winter came. The streets were dirty and the thick fog made it hard for Pocahontas to breathe. She felt tired and would sit by her window with young Thomas and cough and cough. Her chest hurt and her arms and legs ached. Two of her cousins who came to London with Pocahontas also suffered from the foul air. They died during the winter, coughing up blood from their weak lungs.

Pocahontas did not feel like going to fancy homes and parties anymore. She could not breathe in London. The dirty air hurt her throat and chest, and the noise of the many people and smell of the filthy river made her feel sick most of the time.

John Rolfe took her and Thomas away from London, to live for a while in the country, at Brentford. Pocahontas left with her husband and son, feeling tired and weak, and unhappy because she felt her old friend had forgotten her.

Old Friends Meet

THE COUNTRY AIR WAS BETTER FOR POCA-
hontas. She was able to take walks in the
meadow and rest peacefully in the quiet of
the country night. She did not get well, however, and the damp air, even in the country,
made her cough so much that she was weak
and tired.

One day, as she sat with her husband by
the fire in the parlor, she heard a knock at
the door. John Rolfe followed her as she
went to see who the visitor was. It was John
Smith! There he stood, after eight long
years! He laughed and said hello as if nothing had happened since they had last seen
each other.

In the first moments of seeing Captain
Smith's bright blue eyes, Pocahontas must
have remembered how she had thrown herself upon his back and saved him. She must
have thought of the happy days in Jamestown when they had been such good friends.

But then there were the years when she had thought he was dead, and the months she had waited for him to visit her in London.

Pocahontas put her hands up to her face and turned away from Captain Smith. She could not speak to him or even look at him. She was too surprised and too confused. He thought she had forgotten her English, but John Rolfe understood. He suggested that she go to her room, where she could think, and he took John Smith out for a walk.

Pocahontas must have felt both sad and confused as she stood alone in the little room. She had not seen John Smith since that cold and bitter night when she ran through the forest to warn him. Even when her father declared Smith his enemy, Pocahontas had been loyal to Smith because she had made him a member of her family.

She had been a child then, but now she was a married woman with her own child. She had visited the king and queen of England and been entertained by lords and ladies. Nevertheless, John Smith was still her own special family, and she would not forget that.

When her husband and John Smith returned a few hours later, Pocahontas was ready to speak with Captain John Smith.

She spoke to him slowly, in careful English. She was very dignified as she stood before him, looking directly into his eyes.

"You did promise Powhatan," she said, "that what was yours should be his, and what was his, would also be yours. You were a stranger in his land, but you called him father. In your land, I will call you father also."

John Smith knew that Pocahontas was upset with him. Although he had cared for her years ago in Virginia, it was different now. She was married, and it was not proper for them to talk about their past together. He tried to explain that things had changed.

"I cannot be your father here in England, because I am not a king. You are a princess and—"

But Pocahontas interrupted him.

"Weren't you afraid when you came to my father's country? My father was afraid of you also. But I was not afraid. I was not afraid to bring you into our family. Now you are afraid for me to call you father."

She waited a moment, still looking at him. He did not know what to say.

"I tell you then, I will call you father and you will call me child, and I will be forever and ever your countryman," Pocahontas said.

She started to go away from him but then, almost breaking into sobs, said: "They did tell us always that you were dead, and I knew no other. . . . Your countrymen will lie much."

Whenever John Smith had spoken of Pocahontas, he had praised her. He called her "Lady Pocahontas," the "nonpareil" of Virginia, meaning that there was no one equal to her. Although he praised her, perhaps he was uncomfortable being her "father." Perhaps he did not know what to expect from the rambunctious girl who had done cartwheels around the Jamestown fort and had asked him, "Love you not me?"

When he finally saw her, he realized that she had matured into a dignified woman. Perhaps as she spoke to him, he saw that he had been mistaken to wait so long to see her. But as she turned and walked away from him, he was unable to explain his actions.

The two friends who had worked together for peace parted for the last time in sadness.

Gravesend

JOHN ROLFE TOLD POCAHONTAS THAT they must return to Virginia in time to plant the year's tobacco. Pocahontas felt very sick and weak. She did not want to make the journey across the Atlantic Ocean. The ship would be tossed and turned by the spring winds and storms. She and her son, Thomas, would have to stay below in a tiny cabin, where the air would be stale. Her sister Matachanna was also very ill.

They could not wait, John said. They must travel when the winds were right.

In March they boarded the flagship *George* and headed down the Thames River. They went past London with its tall buildings and many people, down to where the river met the ocean, at Gravesend.

It was a lovely spring in England, with lilacs blooming and yellow daffodils growing along the banks of the river. The blackbirds sang in the meadows and starlings flew back and forth with bits of grass and hay in their beaks to build nests.

Pocahontas could hardly smell the fresh lilacs or hear the birds call. She was too ill. John Rolfe knew that she could go no farther and asked the captain to anchor so he could take his wife ashore. Immediately a doctor was brought, but it was too late to save her.

John Rolfe saw that she was dying and brought Thomas to her. They were with her as she spoke her last words.

"All of us must die," she said to John, and then looked at her small son. "He will be your comfort and hope. It is enough that the child liveth. . . ."

As she closed her eyes for the last time, she may have thought of the heaven above the earth that Reverend Whitaker had told her about. Or she may have remembered the sunsets back in her land of Virginia. Once, she had believed that after death she would go beyond the mountains toward the setting sun, where she would dance and sing again with the Indians.

She was never to go back to the land of the Indians. Her body was buried in St. George's churchyard, in Gravesend, England.

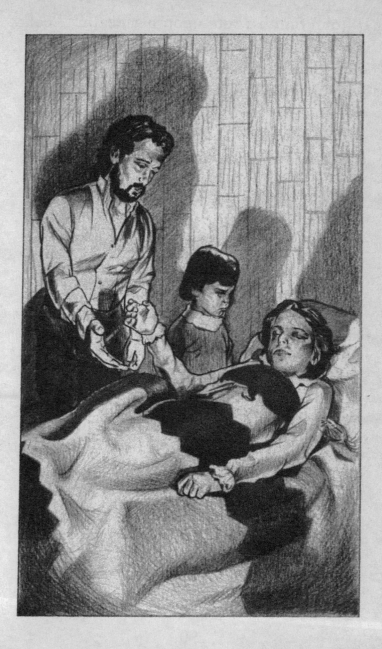

John Smith wrote upon her death: "Poor little maid. I sorrowed much for her thus early death, and even now cannot think of it without grief, for I felt toward her as if she were mine own daughter."

Pocahontas was only twenty-one when she died. She was born in the land of the Indians and was called Matoaka by her family. When she became a part of the white man's world and met with the queen and king of England, she was called Lady Rebecca.

But the world remembers her as Pocahontas, the young girl with the merry eyes and the happy smile of a peacemaker. It was Pocahontas, "little wanton," "mischievous one," who brought joy into a harsh land and peace between hostile men. She was a true princess, a princess of peace and goodwill.

1607 In April Captain Christopher Newport's three ships arrive in the Chesapeake.

In December John Smith is captured by Opechancanough and after a few weeks is taken to Powhatan.

Pocahontas stops John Smith's execution.

1608 Pocahontas begins serving as ambassador for her father, Chief Powhatan.

In May Pocahontas negotiates the release of Indians imprisoned by John Smith.

1609 In January John Smith returns to Werowocomoco to trade with the Indians, and Pocahontas warns Smith that Powhatan is planning to kill him.

Pocahontas saves the life of Richard Wiffin.

Powhatan moves Pocahontas and the rest of his family to Orapaks.

In July John Smith returns to England.

1609–
1610 From October to April "starving time" takes place in Jamestown. Powhatan declares war on Jamestown, and Pocahontas is not allowed to visit the settlement.

1610 Pocahontas is sent to live with the Potomac Indians.

1611 John Rolfe arrives in Jamestown.

1613 Pocahontas is taken hostage by Captain Samuel Argall and is forced to return to Jamestown.

1614 In April Pocahontas and John Rolfe are married.

1615 Pocahontas and John Rolfe's son, Thomas, is born.

1616 The Rolfes sail for England.
During the winter Pocahontas visits London and meets the British royalty.

1617 Pocahontas becomes ill and goes to the countryside in Brentford, England, to recuperate. John Smith visits Pocahontas at her country home.
On March 21 Pocahontas dies and is buried in St. George's churchyard in Gravesend, England.